Science, Maker, and Real Technology Students

S.M.A.R.T.S.

S.M.A.R.T.S. is published by Stone Arch Books
A Capstone Imprint
1710 Roe Crest Drive
North Mankato, MN 56003
www.capstonepub.com

Text and illustrations © 2016 Stone Arch Books

Library of Congress Cataloging-in-Publication Data is available on the
Library of Congress website.

ISBN: 978-1-4965-0465-4 (hardcover) 978-1-4965-0473-9 (paperback)
978-1-4965-2342-6 (eBook PDF)

Summary: Strange things are happening at Hubble Middle School.
Someone's setting off the fire alarm, breaking into the school at night, and
secretly using the school's brand-new 3-D printer. But worst of all, the
S.M.A.R.T.S. are being blamed! Can the team bring the true troublemaker
to justice, or will they be forced to take the fall?

Designer: Hilary Wacholz

Printed in China by Nordica
0415/CA21500550
032015   008838NORDF15

S.M.A.R.T.S.

AND THE 3-D DANGER

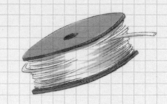

By Melinda Metz

Illustrated by Heath McKenzie

STONE ARCH BOOKS
a capstone imprint

1

"So Watson finds a rock and asks Sherlock what kind it is," Jaden Thompson began as he and his best friends, Zoe Branson and Caleb Quinn, walked into the media center at Hubble Middle School on Tuesday morning. "Sherlock says, 'It's sedimentary, my dear Wat—'"

But before Jaden could finish, a loud shriek came from the back of the room near the makerspace.

"That sounded like Mrs. Ram!" Zoe cried, panicked by the teacher's scream.

Mrs. Ram — short for Mrs. Ramanujan — was more than just the fifth-grade science teacher at Hubble. She was also the sponsor for the school's science team, S.M.A.R.T.S. — Science, Maker, and Real Technology Students. Zoe, Caleb, and Jaden were all in her class, as well as in the club.

"Go!" Jaden exclaimed. "I'll catch up." Because he had cerebral palsy and had to wear leg braces, he couldn't move as quickly as his friends.

Zoe and Caleb raced past the rows of bookshelves and skidded to a stop near the makerspace, the community area at the back of the media center where students could collaborate on ideas, robotics, science, and computers. Mr. Leavey, the school librarian, and Mrs. Ram were both standing there. They looked startled to see the kids skidding to a stop.

"What's wrong? What happened?" Caleb demanded.

"Are you okay?" Zoe asked, looking around to see what might have caused the scream.

"Everything is fine," Mrs. Ram assured them.

"Then why did you scream?" Jaden asked, joining the group.

"It wasn't a scream," Mrs. Ram explained. "It was more like a squeal of excitement. I was blown away by what just arrived for the makerspace!"

"What is it?" Caleb asked.

Mr. Leavey and Mrs. Ram stepped back, allowing the three kids to see what was sitting on the table.

Zoe's brown eyes went wide. "Is that a —"

"It's a 3-D printer!" Caleb burst out, interrupting her.

"It's for us?" Jaden asked. "For S.M.A.R.T.S.?"

Mrs. Ram grinned and nodded. "That's a big yes!"

Zoe started hopping up and down on her toes. Jaden and Caleb did a fist bump. A 3-D printer they were going to be able to use? That was beyond awesome.

"We applied for a grant to get the money for the printer," Mr. Leavey explained, grinning just as widely as Mrs. Ram. "And we got it! Look what I just made."

He opened the Plexiglas door at the front of the printer, reached in, and pulled out a hand made out of red plastic. "It's a copy of my hand!"

"We got a 3-D scanner too," Mrs. Ram explained. "That way we can make copies of real objects — like Mr. Leavey's hand. But there's also software that will let us create 3-D objects on the computer and then print out 3-D versions."

"It's so interesting," Mr. Leavey said. "After I scanned the 3-D image of my hand into the computer, I used a computer program to separate the image into hundreds of horizontal layers. The printer builds the object you're creating one layer at a time. It has a nozzle that moves around, pouring out melted plastic. The plastic hardens almost immediately, so there's no wait time between making layers. Think of it as using an extreme glue gun to draw. When all the layers are combined — voilà!"

Mr. Leavey waved the plastic replica he'd made of his hand. Zoe noticed his shirt had come untucked — again. Typical Mr. Leavey. He always kept the media center in

perfect order, but he had trouble keeping himself quite as tidy.

"That's so cool!" Caleb exclaimed, exchanging an excited high five with Jaden. "I can't wait to try it out."

Zoe smiled, feeling just as pumped as the boys. The three of them loved science, although they hadn't realized how much they had in common until they'd all joined S.M.A.R.T.S. at the beginning of the year.

Just then, Ms. Romero, the school principal, hurried into the makerspace. "You haven't seen my keys, have you?" she asked Mr. Leavey and Mrs. Ram. "I'm sure I had them with me when I came in to take a look at the printer, but I didn't make it back to the office with them."

Mr. Leavey shook his head. "Sorry," he said. "We'll keep an eye out."

Ms. Romero nodded. "Okay, thanks." She turned to the kids and added, "Have fun with your new printer. Mr. Leavey and Mrs. Ram convinced me you'll use it responsibly and learn a lot. Enjoy it." With that, the principal gave a little wave and walked away.

"I know you'll all make me and Mr. Leavey very proud with the wonderful things you make," Mrs. Ram said.

"It's true. You got a 3-D printer!" Barrett Snyder yelled as he raced up to them. His brother Kevin, a fifth-grader like Jaden, Caleb, and Zoe, trailed behind him. "Someone said they saw the box when it was delivered, but I didn't believe it."

Zoe was surprised to see Barrett in the makerspace. He was a sixth grader and hated everything about S.M.A.R.T.S. — mainly because he hadn't been allowed to join. Hubble Middle School rules said a student had to have a C average to be in any of the after-school clubs, and Barrett's grades were too low.

"I saw a show about 3-D printers — you can make anything with them! If you draw it, you can make it. Who gets to use it first?" Barrett asked. He was talking so fast it was a little hard to understand every word.

"The kids in S.M.A.R.T.S. will be using —" Mrs. Ram began.

"Just them?" Barrett interrupted, his mouth twisting into a scowl. "That's not fair! I bet I know as much about science as anyone in that club."

Kevin put his hand on his Barrett's shoulder. "Calm down," he instructed, his voice low and steady. Although he was a year younger, Kevin was acting like the big brother.

Barrett twisted away. "It's unfair!" he exclaimed.

"Barrett's actually been doing better in all his classes," Kevin told Mrs. Ram and Mr. Leavey. "I know you have to have a C average to be in any school clubs, but I bet if report cards came out tomorrow, Barrett would have that."

"I would! That's why it's supremely unfair!" Barrett exploded.

"Barrett, calm down," Kevin said. "I'll handle it."

"Barrett, it's so great that you're improving your grades," Mrs. Ram told him. "We can't let you in the club right now, but when school report cards are released in January —"

"Forget it! I don't want to be in your stupid club anymore!" Barrett interrupted. "I can't stand anyone in it." He spun around and stormed toward the door. "I would have made amazing stuff. You're all going to be sorry."

"He doesn't mean it," Kevin assured them. "He just gets upset." With that, he took off after his brother.

"I wish we could make him understand that we know how good he is at science," Mrs. Ram said, staring after Barrett. "If his grades have really improved, I'd love to have him join S.M.A.R.T.S. after the next report cards come out."

"What do you think he meant when he said that we'd all be sorry?" Caleb asked. "What do you think he's going to do?"

"I'm sure he just said that because he was upset," Mrs. Ram answered. "He's not going to do anything."

Caleb wanted to believe her, but he wasn't so sure she was right. Barrett had sounded pretty serious to him.

NERDS RULE

2

"I can't stop thinking about what Barrett said this morning," Caleb told Zoe and Jaden as they headed to the media center over lunch. They wanted to learn everything they could about the 3-D printer. Maybe there would even be time to try it out! "I think he might really try to do something to hurt the S.M.A.R.T.S. He said we'd all be sorry."

Zoe shook her head. "Mrs. Ram was right. That's just something you say when you're mad."

When they reached the media center, three of the other S.M.A.R.T.S. — Sonja, Benjamin, and Samuel — were already there. Apparently they'd decided to use lunch to check out the 3-D printer too. Mr. Leavey was standing with them.

"Mrs. Ram and I have come up with a challenge for you S.M.A.R.T.S.," the librarian announced. "We think the printer should be something that benefits the whole school. So your assignment is to come up with something you think every student at Hubble Middle School would find useful."

"How big can the something be?" Sonja asked. "I mean, what's the biggest thing the printer can make?"

"It can make an object a little smaller than a shoe box," Mr. Leavey answered. "But you're not limited to that size. You can make multiple pieces and put them together."

"Does what we make have to be red — like the hand you made?" Zoe asked, looking over at the plastic hand sitting on the table next to the printer.

Mr. Leavey shook his head. "Nope. Our printer can only print in one color at a time, but we have a range of colors to choose from." He picked up what looked like a spool of blue wire from the table. "This is a roll of the plastic the printer uses. It's called filament. The printer melts the filament and uses it to create the objects you want printed."

"Cool," Caleb said. "So we could make different pieces in different colors if we want to?"

Mr. Leavey nodded. "You got it — as long as whatever you make is useful to everyone at school. Don't forget that part." He gave the printer an affectionate pat, then looked at his watch. "I need to make a call in my office. Leave the printer off while I'm gone. You can start thinking about what you want to make."

"Useful to everyone at school," Jaden repeated thoughtfully. He wanted to come up with something great.

The S.M.A.R.T.S. were all quiet for a few minutes as they brainstormed. Finally, Caleb broke the silence. "I built an extreme rocket on Minecraft," he said. "With the printer, I could make it for real."

"Oooh! I could make my planet — Ezo!" Zoe exclaimed. Her biggest dream was to become an astronaut and discover a planet. She'd made tons of drawings of what it could look like. She changed her mind a lot about what the name should be, but it was always a word that used the letters of her name — sometimes first name, sometimes middle, sometimes last, sometimes the letters from all of them.

"But neither of those things are useful for *everyone*," Sonja pointed out.

"Oh, yeah," Caleb said, frowning. Even though his rocket was so cool everyone would want to look at it, Sonja was right. It wasn't useful.

Zoe sighed. "Ugh, I guess you're right." Even though she thought all her fellow students would probably want to come to the media center and see her planet.

"My head!" Jaden exclaimed.

"What?" Benjamin and Samuel — also known as Thing One and Thing Two — asked at the same time. They were identical twins and almost always finished each other's sentences. They almost always dressed alike too, which was how they'd gotten their nicknames.

"We could make a model of my head," Jaden explained. "Part of it could be cut away to show my brain and optic nerves and everything. We could paint it to make the colors right."

"How is a model of your head useful to everyone?" Sonja asked, hands on her hips.

Jaden thought for a few seconds. There had to be something. "I know! We could hook it up to a computer. When kids came into the media center they could ask it questions about anything! We could wire it so the mouth opened and closed."

"I think we should make —" Thing One, also known as Benjamin, began.

Samuel opened his mouth, but before he could finish his twin's sentence an ear-piercing alarm sounded —
Breeep! Breeep! Breeep!

The S.M.A.R.T.S. exchanged worried glances.

"Fire!" Caleb yelled.

3

"Fire *drill*," Zoe corrected, speaking loudly to be heard over the alarm.

"But we never have drills at lunch," Caleb argued. "It's the real thing." He was starting to sound upset, which wasn't surprising. Caleb always thought everything was about to turn into a disaster.

Just then, Mr. Leavey hurried back out of his office. "Okay, everybody, let's leave in an orderly way. Don't bother to take your things," he called. "Our closest fire exit is the one in back. Walk straight out and across the baseball field to the sidewalk."

"I wonder where the fire started," Caleb said as they all left the media center. "Maybe in the kitchen or maybe —"

Jaden cut him off. "Know why firefighters always have Dalmatians with them?" He didn't wait for a response. "To help them find a fire hydrant."

Caleb snorted, and Zoe rolled her eyes. "Only two left, Jaden," she warned. She'd given him a three-jokes-a-day limit. Any more of his dumb jokes would make her brain pop.

Jaden just smiled. He'd been trying to get Caleb's mind off the fire drill, and for the moment, it seemed to have worked. But as they passed the Dumpster, a new sound joined the *breep*s coming from the school. *Weee-oooh. Weee-oooh. Weee-oooh.*

"Fire truck!" Caleb shouted, immediately worked up again. "I told you it wasn't a drill!"

"Everybody's getting out," Zoe told him. "We're all going to be okay." But her heart had started beating faster. It *was* a real fire!

When they reached the sidewalk edge of the baseball field, where a large group of students had already gathered, the kids turned and stared at the school building.

"I don't see any smoke or anything," Sonja said.

The sound of the siren got louder, and a few seconds later the fire truck sped by. It turned the corner, heading for the front of the school. The kids all stared at the building. Stared and stared and stared while Caleb muttered, "DOOM," the whole time.

"How long has it been?" Sonja asked.

"I think about twenty minutes," Zoe answered.

"I wish we were in the front so we'd know what was happening!" Caleb exclaimed.

Mrs. Ram overheard him and walked over. "I just came from there," she told the group. "It looks like someone pulled the alarm as a prank — a very dangerous prank. We need to stay out here until the firefighters have checked out the whole building." She moved on to another group of kids to answer their questions.

"I smell nerd," someone said loudly. "It wouldn't be worth it to be in the science club, even with the 3-D printer. I'd come out smelling like nerd."

The six S.M.A.R.T.S. turned around and saw Barrett standing there. Jaden used his stronger hand to smooth

out his T-shirt, which had *#nerd* printed on the front. He bent his head and took a deep sniff. "Smells good to me."

Zoe sniffed her shoulder. "Me too."

Barrett grimaced. "It's like you're proud to be nerds," he said loudly.

A boy standing nearby — Lewis, one of the best math students in the fifth grade —turned. "I prefer the term *more intelligent than you*," he interjected. "But nerd is fine too."

Barrett opened his mouth, shut it, and stalked away in a huff.

"Hey, you guys have the same shirt!" Sonja said, pointing from Lewis's *#nerd* shirt to Jaden's.

"Everybody in the math club just got one," Lewis explained. "Aaron, the president, thought we should all wear the same thing to the Mathematics Olympiad."

"Cool squared," Zoe said.

Lewis smiled. "If any of the rest of you nerds is good at math, you should join. Especially you, Jaden. After all, you already have the shirt."

"S.M.A.R.T.S. keeps us all pretty busy," Jaden said.

"I heard S.M.A.R.T.S. just got the 3-D printer!" Lewis exclaimed. "Being able to create models would really help with some of our geometry problems. Any chance the math club can borrow it?"

"How do you know about it already?" Caleb asked. "We just got it this morning."

"Everybody knows," Lewis said. "At least everybody in math club."

"Mrs. Ram and Mr. Leavey got it for us with a grant," Zoe told him. "I think we get to use it first. Your club could ask, I guess."

"We will." Lewis walked back over to his friends, shouting, "Nerds! Nerds! Nerds!" A few other kids, including some of the S.M.A.R.T.S. and a few members of the Inferior Five, a group of comic-book-obsessed boys, joined in on the chant.

Just then, the all-clear bell rang. Mrs. Ram cupped her hands around her mouth. "Okay, we can go back in. No pushing. No running."

Caleb headed through the back door toward the media center. Suddenly he heard a loud *crrrraaacckk!* and felt something snap under his foot.

Uh-oh, Caleb thought. He looked down and realized he'd stepped on a plastic key ring. Bending down, he picked it up and saw the words *World's Best Principal* under the cracks in the plastic.

"I think I found Ms. Romero's keys!" Caleb announced.

"Oh, right. She was looking for those this morning," Zoe said, walking up behind him.

"They're all sticky," Caleb said. "Or at least one of them is." He inspected the bright-green gunk stuck in the metal groove of one of the keys.

Zoe peered at the key. "I think Ms. Romero has a daughter. It looks like she got some Play-Doh or something in there."

"I'll give them back to Mrs. Ram or Mr. Leavey," Caleb said as they walked back into the media center. "They can return them to her."

"That's weird," Jaden said when they all got back to the makerspace.

"What?" Caleb asked.

"The 3-D printer is on," Jaden replied. "But it was off when we left — wasn't it?"

Zoe nodded. "It was off for sure. Mr. Leavey told us not to turn it on while he was in his office."

"Everybody was outside for the drill, and we're the first ones back here." Caleb frowned. "How could that have happened? What's going on?"

"I don't get it," Jaden admitted.

"I guess someone could have snuck in during the drill," Zoe suggested. "But the fire trucks came and everything. Who'd be stupid enough to want to sneak into a building that might be on fire?"

Nobody said anything. Nobody could think of an answer.

Just then, Mr. Leavey walked into the makerspace. "You all need to head to your next class."

"Okay," Jaden said, "but we might have a problem. The 3-D printer was on when we came back inside. We didn't turn it on — but somebody else did."

Mr. Leavey's brow furrowed, and he looked as confused as the rest of them felt. "Go on to class," he said. "We'll have to figure it out later." He switched off the printer, his frown deepening.

4

Zoe headed to art, her first class after lunch, but it was hard to keep her mind on her project. She couldn't stop thinking about who might have turned on the 3-D printer. Her fingers were itching to make a list of suspects. It would have to be a long list, though. Anyone could have snuck back into the school during the drill.

Ms. McPhee, the art teacher, walked around the classroom, and Zoe forced herself to focus on today's project — making backpack tags. She rolled a piece of bright-green modeling clay between her palms. Once the clay was warm, she shaped it into an oval. She'd already decided to use a Z fridge magnet as a stamp. That way she'd have a tag with her initial on it.

"Is there any more bright-green clay?" Goo, one of the S.M.A.R.T.S., asked. Goo's real name was Maya, but everyone called her Goo because she could answer questions as fast as Google.

"I put a new block on the supply table this morning before school," Ms. McPhee answered.

Goo stood up and headed for the table. Zoe carefully pressed the Z into her clay, then eased it back out. It left a perfect impression behind.

"Does anyone have the bright-green clay?" Goo called from across the room. "There's none over here."

"I don't. I can't even touch clay," Barrett answered, sounding cranky. "My skin will get all red and itchy if I do. I'm allergic. That's why I have to do a stupid collage."

"Next time I'll be sure to get modeling clay without rosin," Ms. McPhee told him. "I didn't realize it was an allergen."

"It's in a ton of other stuff too," Barrett said as Goo returned to her seat with some purple clay. "It's in some dental flosses and the handles of a lot of sports equipment and some makeup and some kinds of chewing gum."

"Barrett should stop wearing so much makeup, then," Antonio, another S.M.A.R.T.S. member, joked as he walked past Zoe and Goo on his way to the sink. As he passed by, he dropped a small folded piece of paper on their table.

Goo opened the note and held it so she and Zoe could both see the note. It said:

Secret S.M.A.R.T.S. meeting tonight.
Back door by the lunchroom at 7.
We have to come up with a present for Mr. Leavey's birthday. No talking until then.
It's a surprise. Pass it on.

"I like to keep it casual in the art room," Ms. McPhee said, walking over. "But you know the rules — no note passing." She plucked the note out of Goo's fingers, tore it up, and stuck the pieces in her pocket.

At least Zoe had gotten to read it first. She definitely wanted to be in on Mr. Leavey's birthday surprise!

* * *

That evening, Caleb crossed the baseball field and walked over to the back door by the lunchroom. He wondered which of the S.M.A.R.T.S. kids had been dumb enough to pick a meeting place right by the Dumpster. It was kind of creepy — and smelly.

Caleb checked his watch — 6:59 p.m. Where was everybody? He looked around, but it was starting to get dark, and all he could see were shadows. The little hairs on the back of his neck stood on end when he heard a rustling sound nearby.

It was coming from behind the Dumpster. Was someone — or some*thing* — hiding back there?

Caleb looked around, but didn't see anything.

The sound came again.

Caleb moved toward the Dumpster as quietly as he could. He didn't want whatever was back there to know he was coming. Cautiously, he peered around the edge . . .

"Hi!"

Caleb almost jumped out of his sneakers. He jerked around and saw Zoe standing there. "Jeez, you scared me!" he exclaimed.

"What were you doing?" Zoe asked.

"I thought I heard something back there," Caleb told her. "Something rustling around."

Zoe shrugged. "Probably a plastic bag." At least that's what she hoped it was. "Do you know who else is coming?"

Caleb shook his head. "The note said not to talk about the meeting, so I didn't."

"Who'd you get it from?" Zoe asked.

Caleb shrugged. "I'm not sure, actually. It was in my locker after lunch. I gave it to Jaden in history, but he can't make it. His family is going to his aunt's house for dinner tonight."

"Well, somehow it got to Antonio. He gave it to me and Goo in art," Zoe said.

"So where is everybody?" Caleb burst out.

"Maybe not that many kids got the note," Zoe answered. "Goo and I couldn't give it to anyone else. Ms. McPhee caught us and tore it up."

Caleb checked his watch — 7:02 p.m.

"Somebody's coming," Zoe answered. Loud footsteps were heading toward the building. She let out a breath when she saw the Things coming around the corner. Sonja appeared a few seconds later.

"Should we start talking about Mr. Leavey's present?" Zoe asked. "I can't stay that long. I told my sister I'd only be about thirty minutes. I'm lucky she only got her license a few months ago. She still loves driving me places."

Caleb nodded. "I told my dad I'd call when we were finishing up. Let's get started. If the person who sent the note is here." He looked at Sonja and the Things.

"It wasn't me," Sonja said.

"Not —" Benjamin began.

"— us," Samuel finished.

"Not me or Zoe either," Caleb told them. "Seems like whoever came up with the idea for the meeting would have gotten here on time."

"Who do you think it was, anyway?" Sonja asked.

"I don't think it was Goo. We were together when we got the note, and she seemed as surprised as I was," Zoe said. "Antonio gave it to us. I guess he could have written it."

"Jaden couldn't have written it. First of all, I'm the one who gave him the note, and second of all, he wouldn't have set up a meeting on a night he couldn't come," Caleb added. "Whoever called the meeting would have planned to be here."

"I agree," Sonja said. "It's weird that whoever wrote the note didn't show up."

Zoe shivered. She told herself it was just because it had gotten cold out there, but really, she was feeling sort of creeped out. Her friends were right. It didn't make sense that someone in S.M.A.R.T.S. would have called a meeting and then not come to it.

"Maybe whoever it was couldn't get a ride or something," Zoe suggested. That made sense. There was no reason to think something bad had happened.

"Or they met with DOOM," Caleb suggested.

Zoe glared at him. Caleb always thought something horrible had happened or was about to happen. It was annoying. "Let's just go," she said. "I'm sure there's a totally normal explanation for why whoever wrote the note didn't show. We'll find out what it is tomorrow."

5

Zoe hurried toward the school building the next morning. She'd gotten there early, the way she, Jaden, and Caleb did most days. They liked to get in some makerspace time before their first class.

As she neared the front steps, someone shouted, "Zoe, wait up!" She turned and spotted Jaden coming toward her.

"Did you find out who sent the note?" Jaden asked when he reached her. Zoe had texted him the night before to fill him in on what had happened — or rather had *not* happened — at the meeting.

"Nope. I texted everyone in the group," Zoe answered. "Nobody in the group wrote the note. Some of them hadn't even seen it."

"Freaky," Jaden said.

"Freaky with creepy sprinkles on top," Zoe agreed. "Why would someone who isn't in S.M.A.R.T.S. call a secret S.M.A.R.T.S. meeting? And then not even bother to show up to it? It makes no sense."

"No reason I can think of," Jaden admitted. "But I'm sure Caleb will be convinced the reason involves DOOM."

Zoe laughed as she held the front door open for Jaden. His impression sounded just like Caleb.

The two friends headed for the media center, but stopped in their tracks when they got a look at the main hallway. The whole thing had been wallpapered in bright fliers. The bright sheets of paper covered almost every locker, plus the trophy case. There were even some taped to the cafeteria door and above the drinking fountain.

"Wowza," Zoe murmured, taking in the scene.

"Lewis and the math club must be really pumped about the Olympiad," Jaden commented.

"Yeah," Zoe agreed. "Cheerleaders have put up this many fliers for football games, but I've never seen a club go so crazy over one of their events. Coolness."

"They must have come in *really* early to get all of these fliers up," Jaden commented.

"Place was like this when I unlocked it this morning," the janitor said as he rolled a garbage can past them. "I'm trying to get them all down before school starts. Principal Romero doesn't want a single one left up."

Before Zoe could ask why the principal didn't want the math club's fliers to stay up, she spotted Kevin coming around the corner. He was carrying an armload of the fliers. As he moved closer, Zoe could see that one of his hands was bright red and covered with blisters.

"What happened?" Zoe asked. "Did you burn yourself?"

"Hives," Kevin said. "They itch a lot, but I'm okay." He turned to the janitor. "I got most of the fliers down from the hallway by the science classrooms. I'll go get the rest."

"Thanks," the janitor answered gratefully. He watched Kevin walk away, then turned back to Zoe and Jaden. "Good kid," he commented. "He saw I wasn't going to be able to get them down in time all by myself and volunteered to help out."

"Why do you have to take them down at all?" Jaden asked, voicing the question Zoe had been wondering about.

"Because whoever put them up broke in," the janitor explained. "I locked the place up tight last night, and there wasn't a single flier in sight. I was the first one here this morning, and when I unlocked the school, they were everywhere. The principal is not happy. We're trying to figure out who did it — and how they got in."

With that, the janitor tugged the garbage can over to the lockers. He started yanking down fliers and throwing them into the trash.

Jaden and Zoe headed toward the media center. They didn't speak until they were sure they were far enough away that the janitor wouldn't be able to hear them.

"I can't believe the math club broke in," Zoe said, shaking her head. "Didn't they know they'd get in huge trouble?"

"How could they not?" Jaden asked. "Breaking in is illegal. Everybody knows that."

As they approached the media center, Zoe heard voices, including a man's voice saying the words *robbery* and *broken lock*. She pressed her finger against her lips, and they crept closer. She wanted to hear more, and she was pretty sure the adults would stop talking if they knew she and Jaden were there.

"I don't understand it. Who would break in just to put up fliers?" the man asked.

"That sounds like Mr. Deegan, my gym teacher," Jaden whispered.

"I'm so relieved that's all they did," another man said. "We've only had the 3-D printer for one day. It would have been devastating if it'd been stolen. The kids are so excited about it."

"That's Mr. Leavey, for sure," Zoe whispered.

"I didn't even think about the printer," Jaden whispered back. "The media center doesn't even have a separate lock. If someone besides the math-club kids had broken in, it could have been stolen."

"I hate that whoever it was got in through the boys' locker room," Mr. Deegan said, sounding angry. "I should have noticed the broken window lock when I was in there yesterday, but the window was closed. I just assumed it was locked like always."

"It's not your fault," Mr. Leavey said. "I would have assumed that too. There was no reason not to."

Mr. Deegan let out a loud sigh. "Breaking in to steal, I get," he said. "But to put up fliers? I just don't understand it."

Jaden shot Zoe a confused look. "Me either," he whispered.

6

"I ran into Lewis in the hallway before English," Jaden announced when he, Caleb, and Zoe sat down at a table with their lunch trays later that day. "He swore the math club didn't have anything to do with the fliers."

Caleb pulled a crumpled #*nerd* flier out of his pocket and spread it out on the table. "Who else would put up signs like this? Remember their shirts?"

"The kids in the math club aren't the only ones with #*nerd* T-shirts," Jaden pointed out. "I wore mine yesterday, remember? If I'd had it on today, I'd probably be in the principal's office right now."

"The math club has the Olympiad coming up. That gives them a motive for putting up the fliers," Zoe commented. "Although the fliers didn't mention the Olympiad."

"Okay, so who else could be a suspect? The kids from the math club should stay on the list, even though they claim they didn't do it," Jaden asked.

"When the math club started doing that 'nerds' chant, the Inferior Five joined in," Caleb said.

"So did some of the S.M.A.R.T.S. who were standing nearby," Zoe pointed out.

"Well, you, Caleb, Antonio, Sonja, and the Things have alibis, at least for part of Tuesday night. You were standing around together behind the school," Jaden said. "Did you see anyone? Or anything out of the ordinary?"

"There was no one else around," Caleb told him.

Zoe snapped her fingers. "Wait a minute — we're not just looking for nerds," she announced. "We're looking for *boy* nerds."

"Boys aren't always the ones who do bad stuff," Caleb shot back.

"That's not what I meant," Zoe said. "This morning Jaden and I heard the gym teacher say that someone messed with the lock on one of the windows in the boys' locker room."

"Oh. Okay. I get it," Caleb said.

"Let's make a list of all the boy nerds. It will help us figure out the best suspects," Zoe suggested.

"Well, we have the Inferior Five and the guys in the math club for starters," Caleb said. "And we should put the boys in S.M.A.R.T.S. on it too since we're all proud nerds."

Zoe started to write.

"My guess is that the lock was broken during last period yesterday. Someone probably would have noticed if had been done earlier," Jaden said. "We need to know which nerds have P.E. last."

* * *

"There's Lewis!" Zoe hissed. She, Caleb, and Jaden had gotten into position near the locker room door as soon as the last bell rang that afternoon. She had the list of nerds out and was putting a star by the names of boys who had P.E. last period.

BOY NERDS

INFERIOR FIVE
- LEO
- OWEN
- RYAN
- MIKE
- GABRIEL

MATH CLUB
- ★LEWIS★
- AARON
- JOHN W.
- JOHN L.
- RICK

S.M.A.R.T.S.

JADEN, CALEB, BENJAMIN, SAMUEL, DYLAN, ANTONIO

Zoe put a star by Lewis's name. "That means Lewis had motive and opportunity," Jaden said.

Caleb looked over Zoe's shoulder, studying what they had so far. But before he could draw any conclusions, the locker room door opened again, and Barrett stormed out.

"I wasn't traveling!" Barrett shouted at his brother, who trailed him out of the locker room. "I was dribbling the whole time!"

"Barrett, calm down," Kevin said. "If you're that upset, I'll talk to the gym teacher. But we won anyway. What's the big deal?"

"I don't like to be accused of something I didn't do!" Barrett kept complaining loudly as they continued down the hall.

"Well, we know Barrett shouldn't get added to the nerd list," Zoe said.

"He's into science and everything, but he acts like *nerd* is the worst insult he can come up with," Jaden agreed.

"I don't even know what Kevin is," Caleb said. "He's too quiet to tell. He could spend all his time gaming or something, but he never says."

"It seems like he spends most of his time trying to control Barrett's temper tantrums," Zoe answered. "You'd think *he* was the older brother, not Barrett. Should I add Kevin to the list?"

Jaden nodded. "Can't hurt. It's better to have everyone who might be a nerd and is in P.E. last period on the list."

They waited a few minutes in case anyone else was still in the locker room. Finally Caleb asked, "Do you think that's everyone? I want to get to S.M.A.R.T.S. I don't want to miss seeing the 3-D printer in action."

"We might have missed a few people who left before we got here, but that should be close to everybody," Zoe answered.

"Let's wait just a couple more minutes," Jaden said. "I want to get a list that's as complete as possible."

About thirty seconds later, the locker room door opened again. Ryan and Gabriel, two members of the Inferior Five, walked out.

"Anybody else in there, you guys?" Jaden asked as the two boys approached.

Gabriel shook his head. "Nope, we were the last two slowpokes," he said as he and Ryan walked away.

"Looks like Ryan and Gabriel get stars too," Caleb said. Zoe nodded.

Jaden studied the list. "And it looks like we have a suspect list. One of the guys with a star by his name is our perp."

7

"It's quiet," Jaden observed as they walked into the media center a few minutes later. Usually there was a lot of talking and laughing during S.M.A.R.T.S. meetings, plus the sounds of tools being used.

"It is," Zoe agreed.

"Good, you're here," Mrs. Ram said when the three of them entered the makerspace. The rest of the S.M.A.R.T.S. members were already there, sitting quietly.

"We didn't want to start without you," Mr. Leavey added, looking serious.

Zoe noticed that all the tabletops were empty. No one was even working on a sketch of something they wanted to make. She, Jaden, and Caleb sat down, and Mr. Leavey cleared his throat. Mrs. Ram looked around the room, then said, "As I'm sure you've all heard by now, we had a break-in at our school last night."

"But the new printer is okay, right?" Sonja asked.

Mrs. Ram nodded. "The printer is fine. But Mr. Leavey and I realized today that some of the plastic filament had been used. Enough to print a small object."

"So the person who broke in last night used our printer?" Antonio asked.

"It appears that way." Mrs. Ram clasped her hands in front of her and stood very still. Usually she paced back and forth as she talked, her ponytail flying.

"The principal and everyone on staff are very concerned about what happened," Mr. Leavey added.

"It's possible that the person or persons go to Hubble," Mrs. Ram said.

Jaden wondered if the adults at school had made their own list of nerd kids who would be likely to put up fliers. Had they thought to look at which boys had P.E. last period? Did they know about the math club's new T-shirts?

"Principal Romero let the police know what happened, and they've questioned everyone who lives in a house with a view of the school," Mr. Leavey said.

"Several of the people they spoke to said they'd seen a group of kids behind the school at around seven o'clock last night," Mrs. Ram said, looking at every kid in turn.

Even though he knew he'd been at the school for a good reason, Caleb felt his face flush when Mrs. Ram's gaze landed on him.

"Now, their descriptions weren't very detailed — height, hair color, that kind of thing. The descriptions could match lots of kids." Mrs. Ram hesitated. "But every description they gave matched someone in S.M.A.R.T.S."

A couple kids cried out, "No!" or, "No way!" But not everyone. The six kids who'd been at the school that night were silent.

"We hate to ask this, but we have to," Mr. Leavey
continued. "Did anyone in this club break into our
school last night?"

This time everyone said, "No."

Mr. Leavey gave a slow nod. "Were any of you at school last night for any reason?"

Caleb had to clear his throat before he could speak, but he was the first to say, "Yes." Zoe, Samuel, Benjamin, and Sonja quickly joined in.

"I wanted to be there, too, but I couldn't," Goo said in a rush.

"Me too," Antonio and Jaden admitted.

"What are you talking about?" Dylan asked from the seat next to Antonio. "Why?"

"We all got a note telling the S.M.A.R.T.S. to meet behind the school at seven o'clock," Zoe explained.

Dylan looked confused. "I didn't get any note."

"We were all *supposed* to get it," Jaden said.

"Who was it from?" Mrs. Ram asked.

"We don't know," Goo said.

"I'm confused," Mr. Leavey said, his forehead wrinkling. "If you didn't know who the note was from, why would you follow the instructions?"

No one said anything. "We expect an answer," Mrs. Ram told them.

Sonja spoke up. "The note said there was a secret S.M.A.R.T.S. meeting to decide what to get Mr. Leavey for his birthday. It wasn't signed. We were supposed to pass the note to everyone in the club, but not talk about it so we wouldn't spoil the surprise for Mr. Leavey."

"We didn't find out until after we met that no one from S.M.A.R.T.S. wrote the note," Caleb added.

"My birthday isn't for three months," Mr. Leavey said. "I'd like to see the note."

Zoe looked down at her lap. "Ms. McPhee caught me reading it in class and tore it up," she said.

"All right," Mr. Leavey said. "If you say you didn't break in, we believe you." He looked over at Mrs. Ram, and she nodded.

"But if any of you think of something later or have something to say that you want to be private, please come talk to us." Mrs. Ram smiled a totally fake-looking smile.

Caleb leaned over to Zoe and Jaden. "Mr. Leavey and Mrs. Ram might believe we didn't have anything to do with the break-in," he whispered, "but witnesses saw us behind the school last night. The principal and the police are going to think we're guilty!"

8

"Calm down," Zoe said. "We explained why we were there, and Mrs. Ram and Mr. Leavey believed us. The principal and the police will, too. We've spent enough of our S.M.A.R.T.S. time talking about the break-in. Now let's get back to the important stuff — what to make with our 3-D printer."

"I looked up some stuff about 3-D printing when I was at my aunt's last night," Jaden added, trying to help distract Caleb. "Somebody used a 3-D printer to make a guitar. And this guy made a bicycle he could actually ride. They both made their projects in pieces and then put them together. So we can think of something big for everyone at school to use if we want to."

"I can't think about the 3-D printer now," Caleb burst out. "Didn't you hear me? The police could be coming to arrest us at any second!"

"The police aren't coming for us," Zoe said. "I'm sure they have other suspects." Just then, an idea hit her. "But what if we don't have *enough* suspects? What if we were wrong when we decided a nerd was behind the break-in?"

"What makes you say that? Why would a non-nerd put up those fliers?" Caleb demanded.

"To put the blame on a nerd!" Zoe explained. "Maybe that's why someone wrote that note to everyone in S.M.A.R.T.S. Maybe they wanted to make it look like *we* are the ones who broke in."

"It's a set up! Somebody's out to get us!" Caleb said, speaking fast.

"Whoa. Hold up. It's possible S.M.A.R.T.S. kids were the target, but we don't know that for sure," Jaden told Caleb.

"Come on," Caleb shot back. "Somebody got a bunch of us to gather at what they knew was going to be the scene of the crime. And they left fliers that practically announced we did it."

"Not us necessarily — there are other nerds at school," Zoe reminded him.

"But not other nerds who were tricked into showing up at school the night the break-in was going down," Caleb argued.

Zoe looked at Jaden. "He might have a point. S.M.A.R.T.S. kids were the ones conned into gathering in back of the school. Not that far away from the window with the broken lock!"

"It's a good theory," Jaden admitted. "But we need to get some evidence before jumping to conclusions."

"I'm telling you, someone's out to get us!" Caleb insisted.

Zoe put her finger to her lips. "*Shhhh*! I don't think we want Mrs. Ram or Mr. Leavey to hear us talking about the break-in right now."

"We need to solve it first," Jaden agreed. "Then we go to them."

"I think we need another list. Instead of nerds, we need to have a list of boys who would want to hurt people in S.M.A.R.T.S. — and who also have P.E. last period."

"Barrett should be on it for sure," Jaden said. "He was really mad about not being allowed in S.M.A.R.T.S."

"And he said he hated everyone in the group. He even said we'd all be sorry!" Caleb added.

"We're forgetting that the 3-D printer was used the night of the break-in," Zoe told them, taking a pen out of her backpack and starting a new list. "Mrs. Ram said enough plastic was used to make a small object. So maybe the break-in wasn't really about us. Maybe someone just wanted to use the printer and thought we'd be easy to blame."

Jaden frowned. "If that's true, then the goal wasn't to get us in trouble. But whoever it was didn't mind setting us up."

"Okay, so I'm making a list of people who want to destroy us. And people who'd want to use the 3-D printer. And for both lists, I'm only naming boys who have P.E. last period, right?" Zoe asked.

Jaden nodded.

"Barrett goes on both lists," Zoe commented.

Caleb looked over her shoulder as she wrote. "What about Lewis?" he asked. "He said the math club wanted to use the 3-D printer. He could have broken the lock so they could get in."

"I guess he should go on the list of suspects who wanted to use the printer," Jaden said. "But Lewis was friendly the day of the fire drill. I don't see him wanting to destroy the S.M.A.R.T.S. I mean, the whole math club backed us up when Barrett tried to insult us."

"And they have those #nerd T-shirts," Zoe said. "The fliers make them look as bad as we do, don't they?"

"Yeah, but I say he stays on the list," Caleb said. "Even though I think Barrett's our guy. He hates us, said he wants to make us pay, *and* he wants to get his hands on our printer."

"Tomorrow we should —" Jaden started to say.

Just then, Mrs. Ram clapped her hands. "That's all the time we have today," she called. "Start cleaning up. And remember, Mr. Leavey and I are ready to talk to anyone who knows something about the break-in."

"We're going to get proof of who broke in," Jaden said, sounding determined. "We're not letting the S.M.A.R.T.S. take the blame."

"Right!" Zoe exclaimed. "We're in S.M.A.R.T.S. for a reason — we're smart. Smart enough to solve this. Whoever did it is going to be sorry they messed with us."

Caleb actually smiled. "Very sorry."

9

When Jaden got to school Thursday morning, there was a crowd gathered in the parking lot.

"Somebody has to go get Principal Romero!" a girl in the crowd exclaimed.

"I'm not telling her about this," a boy answered. "I don't even want to be near her when somebody else tells her."

The boy backed up a little, and Jaden saw it was Lewis. He turned and headed toward the entrance to the school. "What happened?" Jaden called after him.

Lewis didn't stop. "Somebody broke one of the windows in the principal's car," he answered over his shoulder.

Jaden walked over as quickly as he could. He spotted Zoe and Caleb in the crowd and squeezed in next to them. The smashed window was only part of what was wrong. The principal's Toyota had been covered with *Nerd Is the Word* and *#nerd* fliers.

"And we thought we were in trouble yesterday," Zoe muttered.

"This isn't just someone wanting to use the printer who decided we'd be easy to blame," Caleb added. "This is someone wanting to destroy us."

"And there's only one person on the list of people who want to destroy us — Barrett," Zoe said.

Jaden's eyes darted over the brightly colored fliers, the glass on the seat of the car, and the glass on the ground. Something didn't make sense. He looked the car over more carefully, and then it hit him. "This is a prank!" he announced.

"You call vandalizing my car a prank?" Principal Romero asked, striding toward them at that exact moment. Everyone went silent. Some kids started to slink away.

Jaden shook his head. "No, of course not. But the window isn't really broken," he said, explaining what he'd just noticed. "Look, there's glass on the ground and inside on the seat. But if the broken glass came from the window, there should be pieces still stuck in the frame."

"But there isn't," Caleb added, realizing what Jaden had already figured out. "Because the window isn't broken. It's just rolled down."

"So somebody brought the glass and put it on the seat and on the ground?" Zoe said. "Why?"

The principal gestured for the kids still gathered around the car to back up, then opened the car door. "Jaden's right. The window's just rolled down. The glass isn't from my car," she said, carefully running a finger around the window frame.

Jaden, Zoe, and Caleb exchanged a relieved look.

"But I still don't consider this a prank," Ms. Romero added, her tone stern. "I always lock my car. Always. That means someone broke into it. And that person brought broken glass to school. Someone could have gotten hurt. There's nothing funny about that."

Principal Romero stared at the car a moment longer and then seemed to realize the group of kids was standing there staring at her. "Go on inside, please," she instructed. "And watch your step. I'll make sure this glass gets cleaned up."

"Um, Ms. Romero," Kevin said.

"Yes?" she answered.

"I just found a key on the ground," Kevin said, holding up a red key. "Is it yours? Maybe you dropped it and that's how someone got into the car to roll down the window."

Ms. Romero held out her hand. Kevin handed her the key, then walked away along with everyone else. Jaden, Zoe, and Caleb started to follow, but the principal's voice stopped them before they'd gone more than a few steps.

"Jaden, Caleb, and Zoe," Ms. Romero called. They all turned to face her. "Take a look at this key."

The three of them walked back over, and the principal handed the key to Jaden. It was plastic. As soon as he realized that, Jaden was almost certain he knew where the key had come from. He passed the key to Zoe with a pointed look.

Zoe examined the key — red plastic. She tried to hide the panic rising up inside her as she passed the key to Caleb.

DOOM, Caleb thought. *Extreme DOOM.*

"That doesn't belong to me. It's not my car key," Ms. Romero said, taking the key back. "Your new 3-D printer makes plastic objects." She flipped the key over. "Could it have been used to make this key?"

Now that the principal had asked, there was nothing they could do but tell her the truth.

"Yes," they all said together.

10

Less than an hour later, Zoe's name was called over the loud speaker. Caleb's name was next, followed by Sonja's, then Benjamin's and Samuel's, then the rest of the S.M.A.R.T.S. They were all asked to report to the media center immediately.

Zoe stood up and headed out into the hallway, where she ran into Samuel. They exchanged a worried look, then walked the rest of the way to the media center in silence. Zoe couldn't think of anything remotely positive to say, so she figured it was better to keep her mouth closed. Maybe Samuel felt the same way.

When they got to the makerspace, Zoe was glad to see Jaden and Caleb already at their usual table. She hurried over and sat down with them. Mrs. Ram and Mr. Leavey stood nearby.

Zoe looked at Caleb, wondering how he was dealing. He always thought something horrible was going to happen, and now it really was. They were about to get blamed for what had happened to Principal Romero's car. She knew it.

When all the S.M.A.R.T.S. had taken their seats, Mrs. Ram took the red key out of her pocket and held it up. "Have any of you seen this before?"

"Just when Principal Romero showed it to me, Caleb, and Zoe before school this morning," Jaden answered right away.

Everyone else shook his or her head no.

"Mr. Leavey and I are convinced that it was made with our new 3-D printer," Mrs. Ram continued. "A small amount of red plastic was used the night of the break-in. The file that would have shown what was made was deleted, but this key is the right size for the amount of plastic used. It's the right color too."

"The key is to the principal's car," Mr. Leavey added. "I assume you all heard about what happened to it in the parking lot this morning." He got nods and murmured yeses in response.

"Making a copy of a key that doesn't belong to you is serious. Using that key for an act of vandalism is even more so," Mrs. Ram said. She didn't even sound like herself. Her voice was firm, and her eyes were sharp and watchful. "We need you to tell us the truth. Did one of you make this key?"

Everyone started to answer at once. But with so many voices, it was impossible to make out what anyone was saying.

Mr. Leavey held up his hand, silencing them. "Stop. We're going one at a time. Sonja, did you make this key?" he asked.

"No," Sonja answered, her voice smaller than Zoe had ever heard it. Sonja was short, but fierce. She always stood up for herself — loudly.

Mr. Leavey moved from table to table, repeating his question. Each time, he looked directly into the eyes of the student he was speaking to. Zoe, Caleb, and Jaden's table was the last one he came to. So far no one had answered yes.

"Jaden, did you make the key?" Mr. Leavey asked.

Jaden looked steadily back at him. "No."

"Zoe, did you make the key?" Mr. Leavey asked.

She shook her head, and even though she felt like she didn't have any air in her lungs, forced herself to say, "No."

"Caleb, did you make the key?" Mr. Leavey asked.

Caleb shook his head too. "No."

Mrs. Ram looked disappointed. "Mr. Leavey and I have discussed the situation with the principal," she said. "Until we find out who broke into the school and used the printer, we're canceling all S.M.A.R.T.S. meetings."

"No!" Goo burst out.

"That's not fair!" Caleb cried.

"What's not fair is that everyone in the club is being punished. Whoever is responsible should come forward," Mrs. Ram said. "As we said before, anyone can come talk to me or Mr. Leavey in private."

"You can all go back to class now," Mr. Leavey told them.

"What if no one says they did it? What if the break-in is never solved?" Jaden asked.

Mrs. Ram looked at everyone in the makerspace before she answered. "Then S.M.A.R.T.S. will be shut down permanently."

11

"I just want to say thank you for not making us meet by the Dumpster," Sonja said that afternoon when she and the rest of the S.M.A.R.T.S. had gathered by the flagpole. Since they didn't have a meeting after school, they'd all agreed to meet up and work on the case. And they'd made sure to tell everyone about the meeting in person — no notes this time.

"So where should we start?" Zoe asked.

"I have an idea," Caleb said. "We should go door-to-door, the way the police did after the break-in, and talk to everyone who has a view of the school from their house."

"But the neighbors will just say they saw a group of kids — us — by the Dumpster," Zoe protested. "That's what they told the police."

"But we *know* somebody else was at the school that night," Caleb said. "The person who broke in. Maybe one of the neighbors will remember something we can use."

"Okay, let's go in teams. No one goes to a house alone," Jaden said.

The S.M.A.R.T.S. split themselves up into five pairs. Since there were eleven kids, Jaden, Zoe, and Caleb decided to go together.

"Let's meet back here when we're done," Zoe said after they'd figured out which houses everyone would visit. "It shouldn't take that long with five teams."

Everyone agreed, and the teams headed out. No one answered at the first house Jaden, Zoe, and Caleb tried. At the next house, a woman answered, along with a Chihuahua and a Great Dane. The little one was giving high yips, and the big one was giving low, booming woofs.

"I told — quiet!" the woman said to the dogs, "the police — quiet! — everything." She frowned. "I saw — quiet! — you two — quiet, quiet, quiet!" She paused and pointed to Caleb and Zoe. "I saw you two walking across the baseball field toward the school."

"But did you see anyone else?" Zoe asked, almost yelling so she'd be heard. "Maybe later than you saw us? Or earlier?"

"No, I didn't," the woman answered, using one leg to nudge the dogs back as she closed the door with her other hand.

"Maybe we'll have better luck at the next house," Jaden said as they walked away.

Caleb took a deep breath when they reached the door of the next house and knocked. A tall man with a red nose and watery eyes answered.

"Hi," Jaden said. "I know the police probably already talked to you about the break-in at the school, but we wondered if you'd tell us what you saw that night."

"The police didn't — *achoo!*" The man let out a loud sneeze. "Talk to me. Maybe I was — *achoo!* — asleep. I work — *achoo, achoo!* — nights. Usually I'd be asleep right now, but this cold is keeping me awake."

"So you weren't home Tuesday night," Jaden said, disappointment washing through him.

The man shook his head. "I leave for work at about six in the evening and get home — *achoo!* — around five in the morning. Wednesday morning when I was about to pull into my driveway, I saw — *achoo!* — a boy — *achoo!* He crossed the street right in front of my car — *achoo!* — and headed toward the baseball field. It was really early — *achoo!* Around dawn."

"What did he look like?" Caleb asked.

Through his sneezes the man gave them the boy's description — blond, wearing jeans, around the same age as the three of them.

"So our perp didn't break into the school at night," Caleb said as they walked away, armed with the new information. "That's why we didn't see anybody when we were conned into meeting up behind the Dumpster. He waited till early the next morning."

"I bet none of the other witnesses were up that early," Zoe added. "That's why no one else reported seeing a kid heading across the baseball field around dawn."

"That's a pretty brilliant plan," Jaden admitted. "Whoever it was made sure the S.M.A.R.T.S. were hanging around the school at a time when a lot of people would see them. Then he broke in at a time when most people were still snoozing."

"How many blond boys who wear jeans do you think there are at our school?" Zoe asked as they hurried back to the flagpole.

"Doesn't matter," Jaden answered. "All we need to know is how many blond boys are on our lists of possible suspects."

Zoe studied the lists while they waited for the others to return. "We've got Lewis from the math club; he has brown hair. We've got Ryan from the Inferior Five; he has black hair. We have Gabriel; he has red hair. And we have Barrett, who has blond hair!"

"I knew he was the perp!" Caleb said. "He told us we were going to be sorry, and then he made sure we were! And he got to use the 3-D printer before anybody else."

"We still need proof," Jaden reminded him.

Just then, Benjamin, Samuel, Sonja, and Goo returned to the flagpole. "We got nothing," Sonja announced. "No one saw anything they hadn't already told the police."

"Doesn't matter. One of the people we talked to wasn't home to talk to the police. And he saw a boy who —" Jaden began.

"He saw a boy who was Barrett heading into school really, really early Wednesday morning!" Caleb interrupted.

"*Maybe* Barrett," Zoe corrected. "I know how we can find out. Does anyone have a picture of him?" She pulled out her phone to search; so did the others.

"Got it!" Goo announced after a moment. "I have a picture of Barrett from last year's science fair. Kevin's display was next to mine, and one of my pictures has Barrett and his parents looking at my exhibit."

"Can I borrow your phone?" Caleb asked. As soon as Goo gave it to him, he took off. Zoe and Jaden started after him. When they caught up with him at the house they'd just left, the man was already studying the picture.

"It looks — *achoo!* — a lot like him. *Achoo!*" he said.

Zoe, Jaden, and Caleb exchanged grins. They were close to solving the case!

"But the boy I saw was thinner," the man said. "That kid — *achoo!* — is like a little linebacker."

The kids thanked the man for his help, then turned and headed back in the direction of the school. "We don't have any suspects left," Jaden said, sounding defeated.

"We know a blond boy was walking toward the school before anyone else got there on Wednesday morning," Caleb answered. "If we want to save S.M.A.R.T.S., we have to find him!"

12

"Let's start from the beginning and go over everything we know," Jaden said when he, Zoe, and Caleb met up at the flagpole before school on Friday. Normally they would have met in the media center, but Zoe insisted it would make her too sad to be that close to the makerspace when they weren't allowed to use it.

"Okay, the very first thing was the S.M.A.R.T.S. kids getting that fake note telling us to meet behind the school," Zoe said.

Jaden shook his head. "Actually, the first thing was the printer getting turned on during the fire drill. It was turned off when we left the makerspace, remember?"

Zoe nibbled her bottom lip. "So that means the first thing was really somebody setting off the fire alarm."

"And even before that, the principal lost her keys. I'm going to make a timeline for us," Caleb said. "There's a lot to keep straight."

Jaden looked over the timeline when Caleb had finished it. "That looks like everything."

Zoe nodded. "I want to go pick up the backpack tag I made in art," she told the boys. "Ms. McPhee said she'd bake them last night and be in her room early if we wanted to get them. You want to come with me?"

The boys nodded and followed Zoe to the art room. She hurried inside and looked for her backpack tag on the table by the supply closet. It was easy to spot since she'd made it neon green.

Zoe grabbed it and returned to Caleb and Jaden. "Check it out," she said, showing them the tag with the Z stamped into it.

"Sweet. How'd you make that?" Caleb asked.

"Pressed a fridge magnet letter into the clay before it was baked," Zoe explained.

Jaden didn't say anything. He just blinked rapidly as he stared at the backpack tag. It was making him think of . . .

"The sticky stuff!" Jaden burst out.

"Huh?" Caleb said.

"Zoe's tag is the same color as the sticky stuff that was stuck in the groove of Principal Romero's key when you found it," Jaden said. He turned to Zoe. "You thought maybe her daughter got Play-Doh on it, remember?"

"You think the green sticky stuff is a clue?" Zoe asked.

"I think it could be," Jaden said. "And I think the fact that the sticky stuff is the same color as clay from an art class at our school could be another clue."

"The red key!" Zoe exclaimed. "Whoever broke in used the printer to make the plastic key. But they couldn't have made a key that *worked* unless they scanned the original into the 3-D printer."

"Right!" Jaden exclaimed. "We were pretty sure we knew *when* the key was made, but we didn't think about *how*."

"I returned the principal's keys to her right after the fire drill on Tuesday," Caleb said. "So whoever made the copy of the car key couldn't have had it when they used the 3-D printer Wednesday morning."

"The green sticky stuff *was* clay!" Zoe said. "I bet somebody pressed the key into the green clay. Then later, they used the 3-D scanner to scan the image of the key in the clay. They didn't need the key with them. All they needed was the clay!"

"Genius," Jaden breathed.

"Evil genius, you mean," Caleb muttered. "Whoever made that key is the one who got S.M.A.R.T.S. shut down. I bet he set off the fire alarm too! He could have used the time when everyone was out of the school to get the clay and make the impression of the key. I found the key when we were coming back inside — and the principal lost them that morning. The perp could have had them that whole time."

"But we still don't know who *he* is," Zoe said.

"I was so sure it was Barrett." Caleb curled his hands into fists just thinking about the way Barrett had threatened them when he'd found out he couldn't join S.M.A.R.T.S. until report cards came out. "Do you think that man could have been wrong about the size of the boy he saw? He said it was really early in the morning, before it got very light."

"Yeah, but even though it was early, the boy walked right in front of that guy's car. He saw him up close," Jaden reminded Caleb.

"And even if he did get the boy's size wrong, it couldn't have been Barrett," Zoe said. "He's allergic to modeling clay. He can't touch it. It gives him hives. He didn't even make one of the backpack tags."

"Besides, Barrett has an alibi for the time we think the perp was using the clay to make an impression of

Ms. Romero's car key," Jaden added. "He was outside insulting us during the fire drill, remember?"

Caleb groaned in frustration. "We've figured out so much, but we still have no idea who the perp is! What are we going to do?"

"We're going to keep calm," Jaden told him. "And we're going to figure it out. There's no other option. Let's go over everything again — lost keys, fire drill, keys with green clay, 3-D printer left on, fake-out note, broken lock, break-in, fliers, enough plastic used to make a key, prank on principal's car, Kevin finds a plastic key —"

Jaden stopped abruptly as something dawned on him. "You know who looks like Barrett but smaller? Kevin!"

"Kevin? Why would he want to take down S.M.A.R.T.S.?" Caleb asked. "You're always talking about motive — he doesn't have one."

"What if he did it *for* Barrett? Kevin's always trying to fix things for him," Jaden answered. "He was the one who told Mrs. Ram and Mr. Leavey about how Barrett's grades were improving, remember? He was trying to get Barrett into S.M.A.R.T.S."

"And since he couldn't get Barrett into S.M.A.R.T.S., Kevin decided to destroy it!" Caleb exclaimed. "He made absolutely sure Principal Romero saw the plastic key. He's the one who handed it to her!"

"The day Kevin was helping throw away fliers, I thought his hand had a burn on it," Zoe remembered. "He said it was hives — like what Barrett said he'd get if he touched the modeling clay. Maybe Kevin has the same

allergy. They are brothers, after all. And if Kevin is our perp, he definitely touched clay."

"Why would Kevin help throw away the fliers, though?" Caleb asked. "If he's guilty, he's the one who put them up in the first place."

"Because he's an evil genius, and he knew it would make him look innocent," Zoe offered.

"The hives and the motive are good," Jaden agreed. "But we don't have real proof yet."

Zoe smiled. "I think I know a way to prove Kevin's guilty — we'll need a little help from Mr. Leavey, though."

13

That afternoon, Zoe, Caleb, and Jaden watched from their hiding place behind a row of books as Mr. Leavey led Kevin into his office. They'd told Mr. Leavey about their plan at lunch, and he'd agreed to take part, but they'd had to wait all day before putting it into action. Finally, it was go time!

Zoe, Caleb, and Jaden crept up to the librarian's office door, which was open a crack, and peered in. Mr. Leavey probably wouldn't be happy about them spying, but they couldn't resist. They'd come up with the plan to get Kevin to confess, and they wanted to see if it worked.

"Do I have a late library book or something?" Kevin asked.

"No, it's nothing like that," Mr. Leavey answered. "I wanted to talk to you about this." He held up a block of neon-green clay with the imprint of a key pressed into it — Zoe's house key, but Kevin wouldn't know that.

"But that was in —" Kevin stopped abruptly. "What is it?"

"I think you know what it is," Mr. Leavey said. "The clay had fingerprints on it. We were able to compare them to the fingerprints we have on file from the day the police visited and took prints as part of their demonstration."

Zoe and the boys exchanged knowing looks. Mr. Leavey was turning out to be a great actor! It sounded completely believable that he'd found the clay Kevin had used to make an impression of the key. But in reality, the clay Mr. Leavey was showing Kevin was a new block from the art room. It didn't have Kevin's fingerprints on it at all!

"Th-that's b-because I used the clay," Kevin stammered. "I was h-helping Barrett with his art p-project. Someone m-must have t-taken it l-later."

"He's freaking out," Caleb said, in a gleeful whisper. Jaden and Zoe grinned.

"Really?" Mr. Leavey asked. "Because it was my understanding that you and your brother are allergic to the rosin in modeling clay. That's what Ms. McPhee told me. In fact, Barrett was given a different project."

"Oh, um, I guess it wasn't for school. I heard about what they were doing in, uh, art and decided to try it. My allergy isn't that bad," Kevin tried to explain.

Jaden inched a little closer to the door. Mr. Leavey was about to get to the good part!

"Kevin, a neighbor saw you heading toward the back of the school very early Wednesday morning. You walked right in front of his car when you crossed the street. I think we'll also find your fingerprints on the broken lock on the window in the boy's locker room," Mr. Leavey said calmly. "Unless you wore gloves."

"Yeah, I did," Kevin said quickly.

Zoe and Jaden looked at each other in amazement. Kevin had just admitted he was behind the break-in!

Before anyone could stop him, Caleb charged into Mr. Leavey's office. "You committed a crime just to get back at S.M.A.R.T.S. for not letting Barrett in!" he yelled at Kevin.

Kevin jerked his head toward Caleb. "It wasn't fair!" he exclaimed. "Barrett loves science and technology just as much as you guys. And he's good at it! He should be in the club. His science and math grades are off the charts!"

"You set us up and —" Caleb began.

Mr. Leavey held up his hand. "I'm handling this, Caleb," he said sternly. He turned back to Kevin. "What you did is very serious. Setting off the fire alarm when you knew there wasn't a fire is illegal. And, of course, so is breaking into the school."

Kevin slumped down in his chair. "I didn't plan to do it. But Barrett was so upset when he found out the 3-D printer was only for S.M.A.R.T.S. He's been trying to convince our parents to buy one. My dad is always losing his keys, and Barrett keeps telling him how he could scan his keys in and make copies whenever he wanted to. And then I found the principal's keys right after you told Barrett he couldn't be in the club."

"Barrett can't join S.M.A.R.T.S. *yet*," Mr. Leavey said. "If his grades are up in January, he'll be welcome to join."

Kevin seemed eager to tell them everything now that he'd been caught. "I knew I could use the printer to make a copy of the principal's car key, and I figured I could use that to do something that would get everyone in S.M.A.R.T.S. in trouble." He shot an angry look at Zoe, Jaden, and Caleb.

"Why didn't you just make a copy of the key during the drill?" Caleb asked. "Why did you have to break in? Scanning the key would have taken less time than making the impression of it in clay."

"I turned the scanner on and tried to figure out how to work it, but I wasn't fast enough," Kevin admitted. "I had to ask Barrett a bunch of questions later. But he didn't know why I was asking!"

"And since you had to break in to make the key, you figured you'd blame us for that too," Jaden said.

"Yeah," Kevin admitted. "I saw you wearing that #nerd T-shirt and figured I'd use that. When people at school see the word nerd, they think of you guys."

"Thank you," Zoe said, grinning. "Nerds are the coolest."

Mr. Leavey stood up. "We need to go see Principal Romero. You're going to tell her everything you just told us," he said.

Kevin rose and followed Mr. Leavey out of the office.

"Mr. Leavey did great," Jaden said. "He was just like Sherlock Holmes."

Zoe clapped her hands. "You guys, we just saved S.M.A.R.T.S.!"

14

"It's almost done!" Zoe announced as the nozzle of the 3-D printer moved back and forth, adding layer after layer.

It had been almost a week since Zoe, Jaden, and Caleb had cracked the case of the break-in. Kevin had been suspended for what he'd done, and the S.M.A.R.T.S. had been cleared of any wrongdoing. Now that the club was officially back in action, they'd spent most of the week working on their assignment — creating something useful for the whole school. Now it was time to show it off.

"I'll go get Mr. Leavey," Goo volunteered, heading for the office.

"He's going to be thrilled," Mrs. Ram said. "You all did an awesome job!"

When the printer stopped, Caleb opened the front door and picked up the small plastic object. The rest of the project was already done.

"I hear there is some kind of surprise out here," Mr. Leavey said when he and Goo came back into the makerspace. Somehow the knot in his tie had moved almost to the bottom.

"This is —" Benjamin began.

"— the first part," Samuel finished for his twin. He handed Mr. Leavey a piece of plastic chain link. Each link had been made using the 3-D printer, and each one was a different color.

"And here's the second part," Sonja said. She rushed over to Mr. Leavey and handed him the lock they'd

designed using the computer software and brought to
life with the 3-D printer.

"It's beautiful," Mr. Leavey said, smiling.

"And of course you'll need this," Zoe added, handing
Mr. Leavey the key they'd made. They'd designed it on
the computer too.

"Even though nothing was taken or damaged during
the break-in, we decided the media center needed a
security system," Jaden said.

"You can wrap the chain around the handles of the
double doors, then put on the lock," Caleb explained.

"Thank you. Thanks to all of you," Mr. Leavey said.
"I'm going to use it tonight!"

"We also talked about how there are students who
aren't in S.M.A.R.T.S. but who would love to use the
makerspace and our printer," Mrs. Ram said. "Students
who would use the printer in a responsible way to learn."

"We thought maybe they could use the space and
the printer when S.M.A.R.T.S. isn't using it," Jaden
explained. "We could make copies of the key for you

to give to other teachers and club sponsors. That way if other kids or another club wanted to stay late, the teacher or sponsor could lock the media center when they left."

"I could chaperone kids who aren't in S.M.A.R.T.S.,"
Mrs. Ram offered. "I'd be willing to do that once a month
or so."

"That way Barrett could use the printer," Zoe added.
"He didn't have anything to do with the break-in. And

maybe if he got to do something he loved, like work in the makerspace, he'd be a little nicer!"

"You did it!" Mr. Leavey cried. "I'm so proud of all you. You came up with something that will be useful to everyone at school. Every kid who wants to use the makerspace will be able to, and the 3-D printer and all our other equipment will be safe."

Zoe smiled. "Nobody will be able to use our printer to help them commit a crime ever again. No more 3-D danger!"

NERDS RULE

About the Author

Melinda Metz is the author of more than sixty books for teens and kids, including *Echoes* and the young adult series Roswell High, the basis of the TV show *Roswell*. Her middle-grade mystery *Wright and Wong: Case of the Nana-Napper* (co-authored by the fabulous Laura J. Burns) was a juvenile Edgar finalist. Melinda lives in Concord, North Carolina, with her dog, Scully, a pen-eater just like the dog who came before her.

About the Illustrator

Heath McKenzie is a best-selling author and illustrator from Melbourne, Australia. Over the course of his career, he has illustrated numerous books, magazines, newspapers, and even live television. As a child, Heath was often inventing things, although his inventions didn't always work out as planned. His inventions still only work some of the time . . . but that's the fun of experimenting!

Glossary

accuse (uh-KYOOZ) — to say a person has done something wrong or illegal

alibi (AL-i-by) — a claim a person makes saying that they cannot be guilty of a crime because they were somewhere else when it happened

assume (uh-SOOM) — to believe or think something without first checking that it is actually true

confess (kuhn-FESS) — to admit something, usually something you did that was wrong

con (KON) — to trick

devastating (DEV-uh-stay-ting) — shocking and saddening

hives (HIVZ) — an itchy rash that appears on the skin, usually from an allergic reaction

impression (im-PRESH-uhn) — the shape that is left behind after an object has been pressed into something soft

motive (MOH-tiv) — the reason why a person did something

rosin (ROZ-in) — the sap from pine and spruce trees; used in a variety of products because of its stickiness

suspect (SUHS-pekt) — a person who might have done something wrong and is being investigated

vandalize (VAN-duh-lahyz) — to purposefully damage or destroy property

witness (WIT-ness) — a person who saw something happen

Discussion Questions

1. It's not fun to feel left out of a group, but Barrett and Kevin shouldn't have been so mean to the S.M.A.R.T.S. Have you ever not been allowed to join a group? Talk about how it made you feel and what you did about it.

2. Do you think that Principal Romero's actions were fair to the S.M.A.R.T.S.? Discuss how you would've handled the situation if you were her.

3. Kevin is a very caring brother, even if what he did was not okay. Discuss some ways you help your siblings. How do they help you? If you don't have brothers or sisters, discuss how you help your friends.

Writing Prompts

1. The S.M.A.R.T.S. were given an assignment to make something useful for the entire school. Write a paragraph about something that would be helpful for your school to have and why. You can make up a new invention or write about something that already exists.

2. When Barrett tried to tease some of the kids, he discovered they didn't mind being called nerds. They were proud of their interest in things like math, science, and comic books. Write a paragraph about something you're interested in and proud of.

3. What Kevin did wasn't a good way to solve Barrett's problem. Make a list of other things he could have done to help Barrett feel better.

3-D Printing

A 3-D printer is a type of machine that is able to create a real, three-dimensional object layer by layer. In order to print something, you first have to scan a 3-D image of something that already exists, or create your own 3-D model using a special type of computer software. Those models are then broken into very tiny horizontal layers, and the 3-D printer creates each layer, one on top of the other, until the object is complete.

Although 3-D printing may seem like the stuff of science fiction, the technology has actually been around since the 1980s. Up until recently, 3-D printers were mainly used by manufacturing companies to make quick prototypes, a kind of test object to make sure an idea works before making more. But as 3-D printers have developed and became faster and cheaper, there's been a growing interest in the technology for individual use. Now people (and schools!) can have their own 3-D printers.

Lots of materials can be used in a 3-D printer. For most printers that a individual would own, a plastic is used to print the objects. More advanced printers can use metal, nylon, chocolate, and hundreds of other materials. But one of the most exciting materials a 3-D printer can use is human tissue in a process called bio printing. Although there is still a lot of research that has to be done, doctors may one day be able to use 3-D printers to create new organs for people who need transplants, saving many lives.

More adventure and science mysteries!

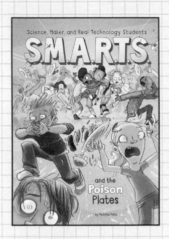
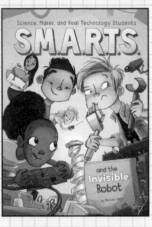